MARVEL

CAPTAIN AMERICA

HIGH-STAKES
HEIST!

Based on the stories by Marvel Comics
By Courtney Carbone
Illustrated by Michael Borkowski and Michael Atiyeh

MARVEL
marvelkids.com

A GOLDEN BOOK · NEW YORK

 Published in the United States by Golden Books, an imprint of Random House Children's Books, a division of Random House LLC, 1745 Broadway, New York, NY 10019, and in Canada by Random House of Canada Limited, Toronto, Penguin Random House Companies. Golden Books, A Golden Book, A Little Golden Book, the G colophon, and the distinctive gold spine are registered trademarks of Random House LLC.
randomhouse.com/kids
ISBN 978-0-385-37426-2
Printed in the United States of America
10 9 8 7 6 5 4 3 2 1

Early one morning, the super hero Captain America and his sidekick, Bucky Barnes, were on patrol at the US Mint in Washington, DC.

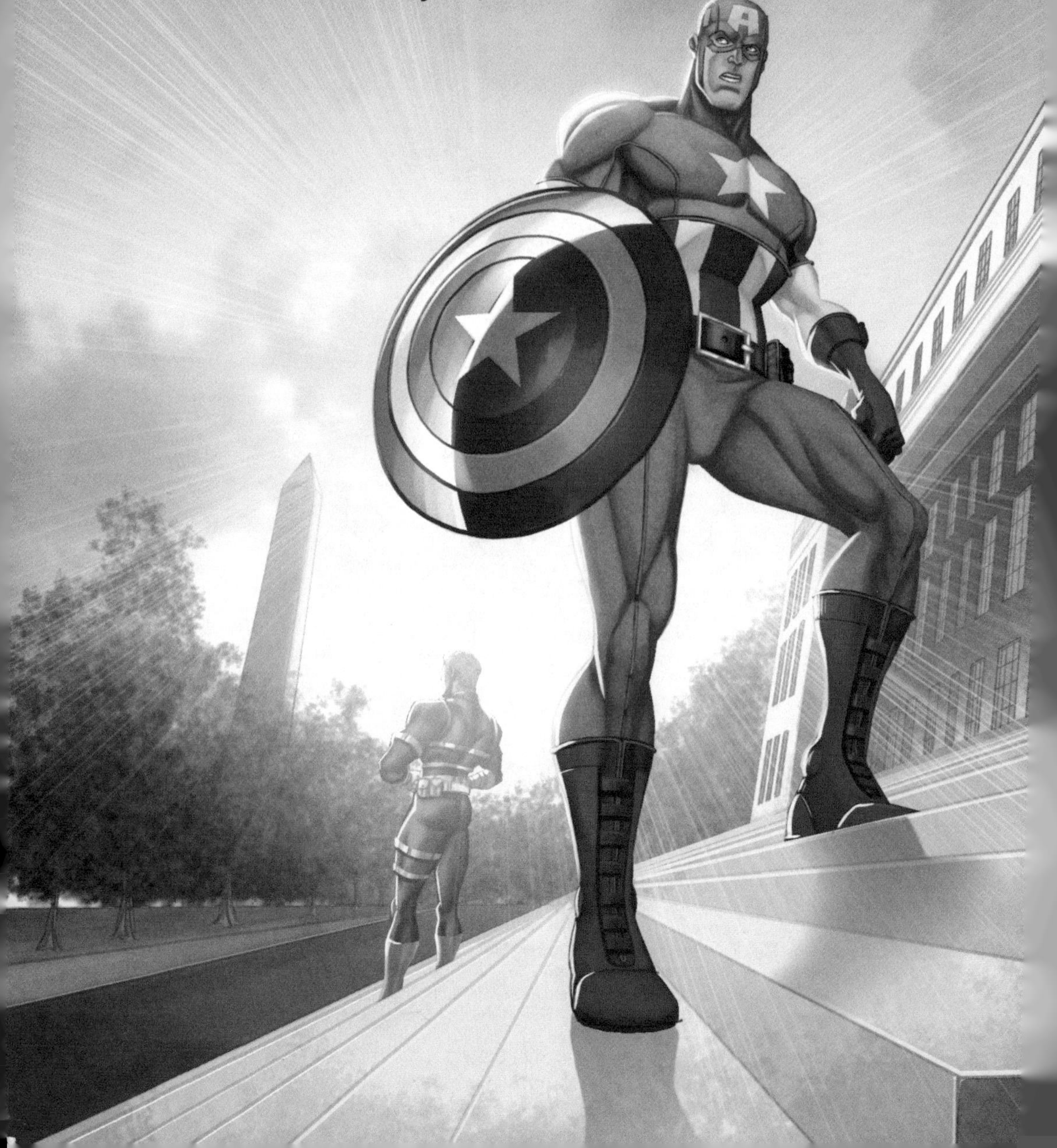

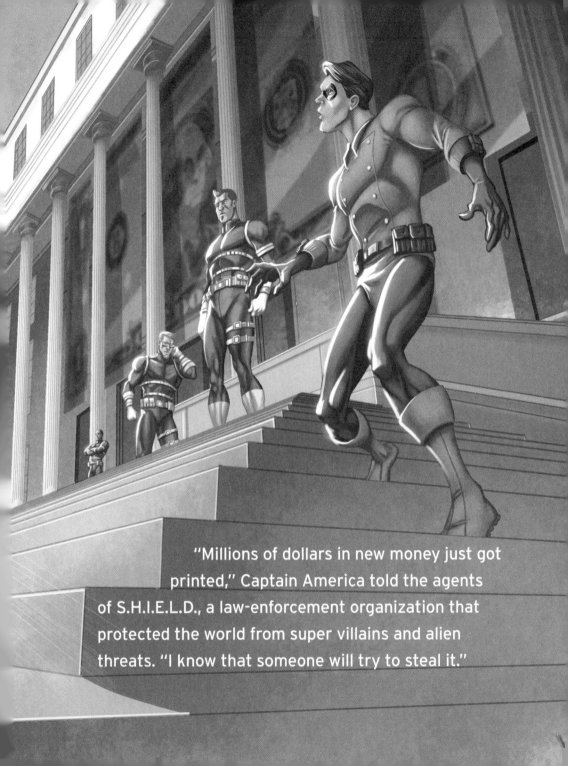

"Millions of dollars in new money just got printed," Captain America told the agents of S.H.I.E.L.D., a law-enforcement organization that protected the world from super villains and alien threats. "I know that someone will try to steal it."

Suddenly, energy blasts erupted from the sky! Moving swiftly, Captain America used his indestructible shield to protect Bucky.

"Quick! Get behind me," Captain America shouted.

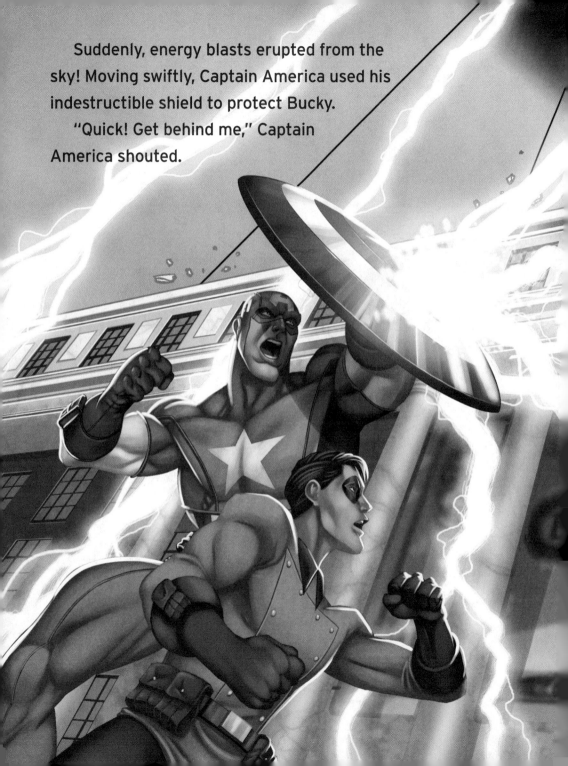

"Cap, I saw something on the roof," Bucky said.

"Let's go," Captain America replied.

The heroes dashed into action.

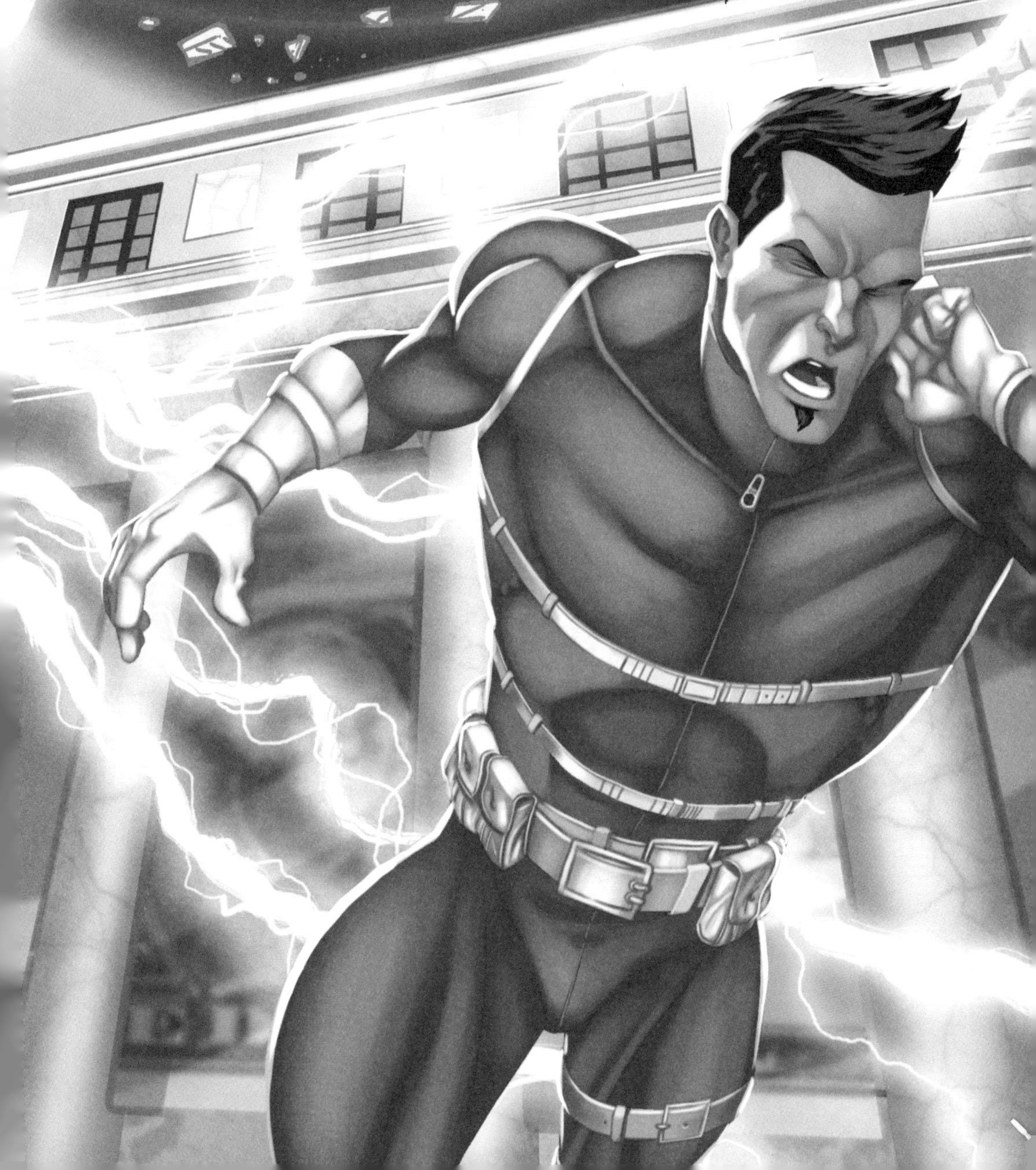

"The doors are locked from the inside," said Bucky.

"Follow me!" Captain America shouted as he began to climb the building.

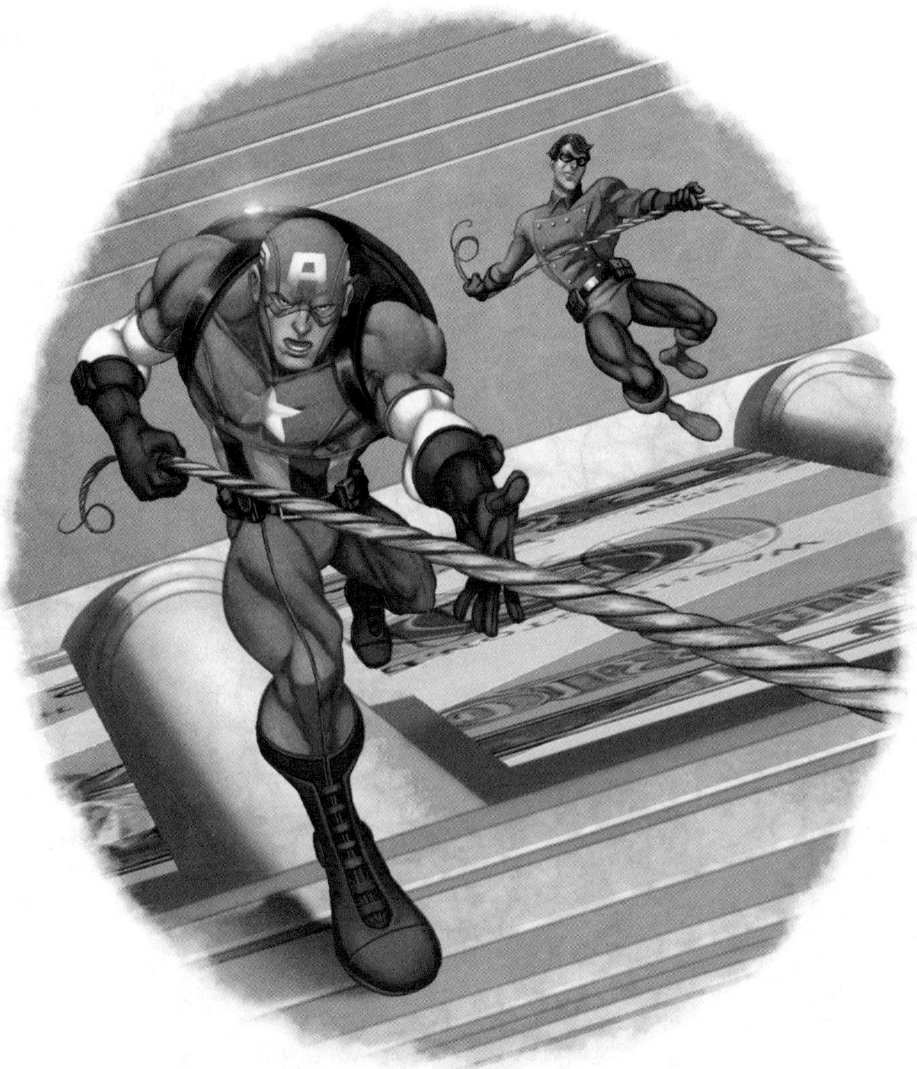

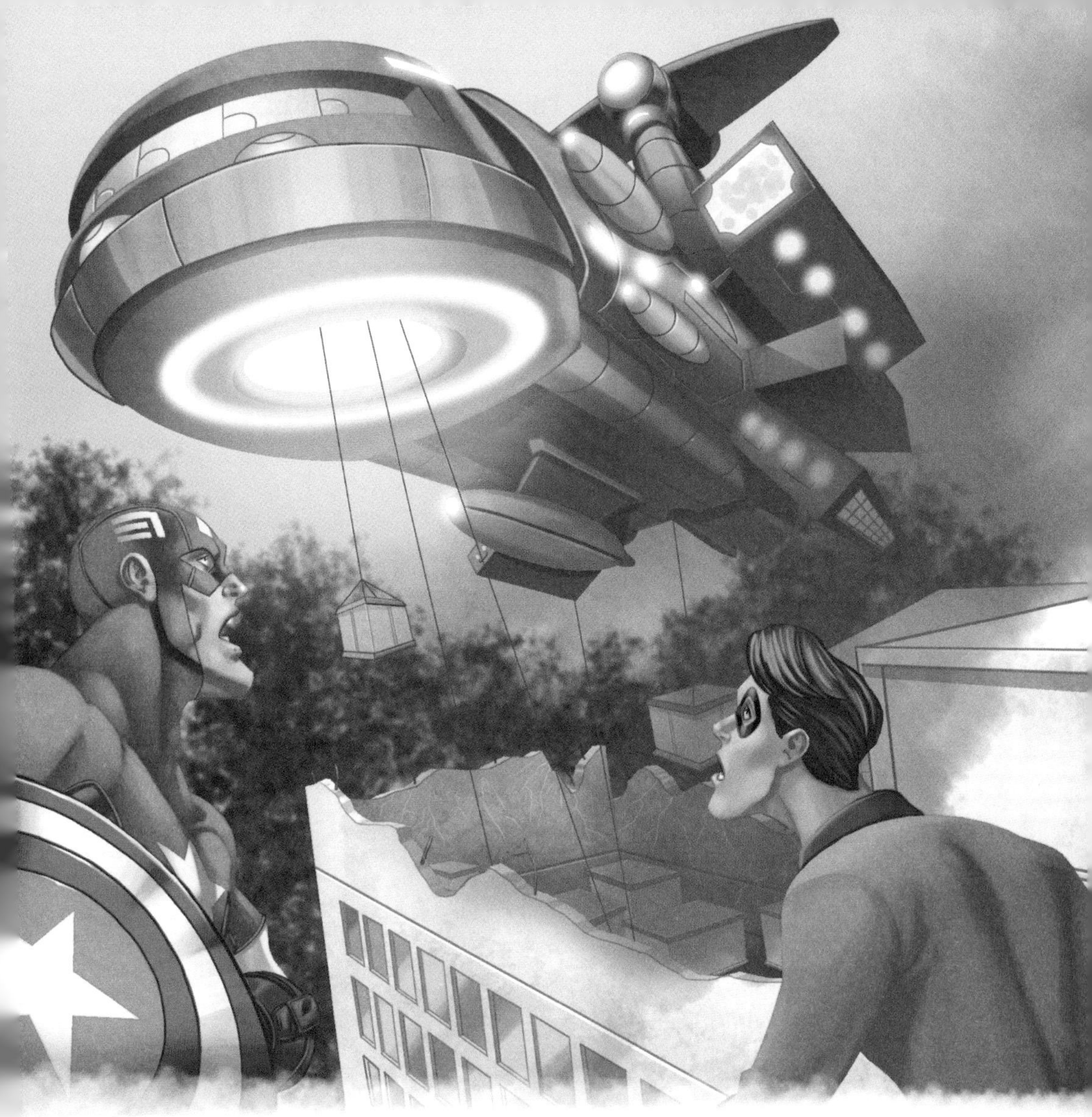

"They tore off the roof!" Bucky exclaimed.

"Somebody really wants those new bills," Captain America said. "Let's find out who it is—and stop them!"

"Get every last dollar," a robotic villain barked at his monster-men. "I will use these riches in my plans to take over the world!"

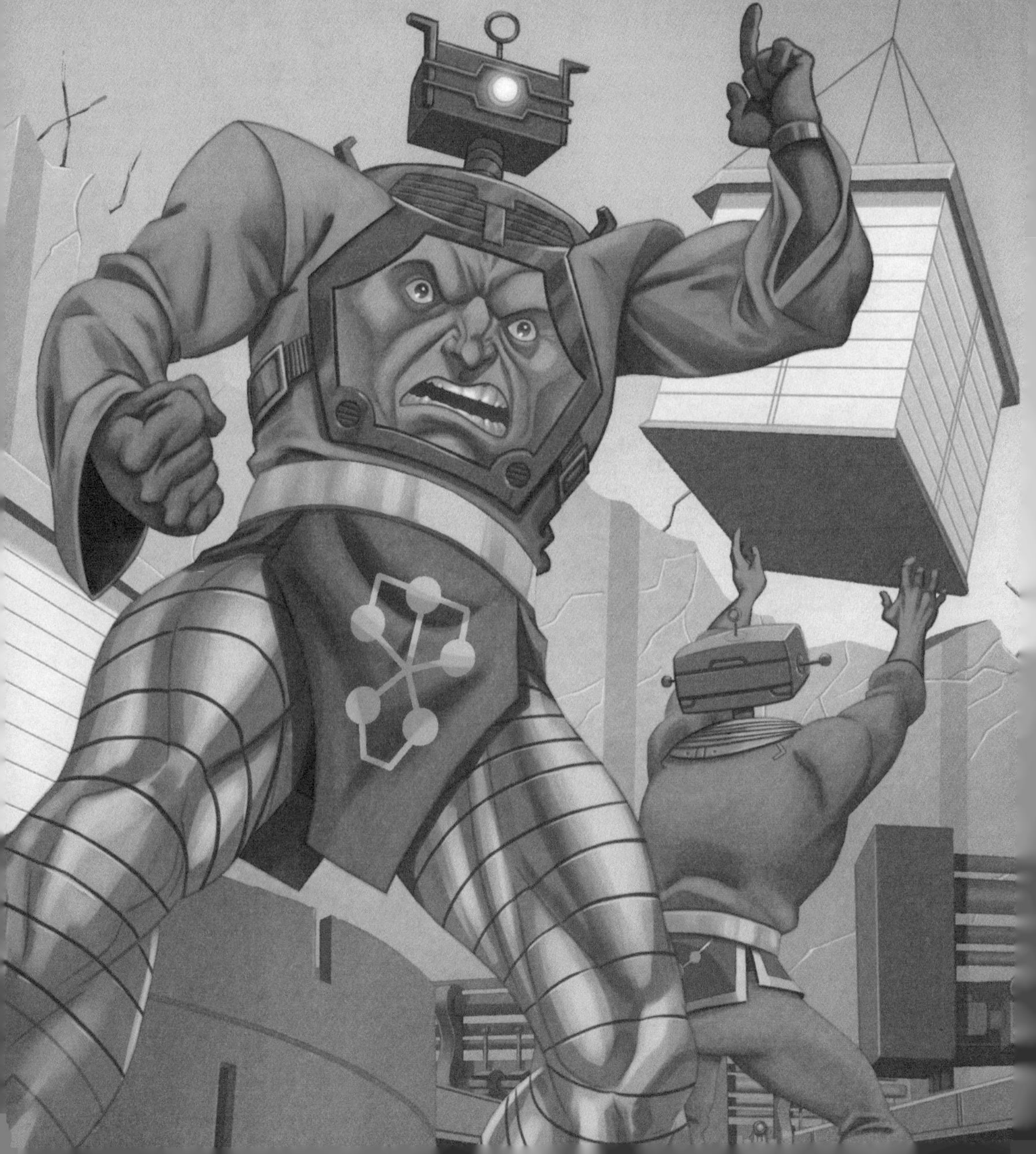

"You're going to have to put your money where your mouth is, ARNIM ZOLA!" Captain America shouted. "Because the buck stops here!"

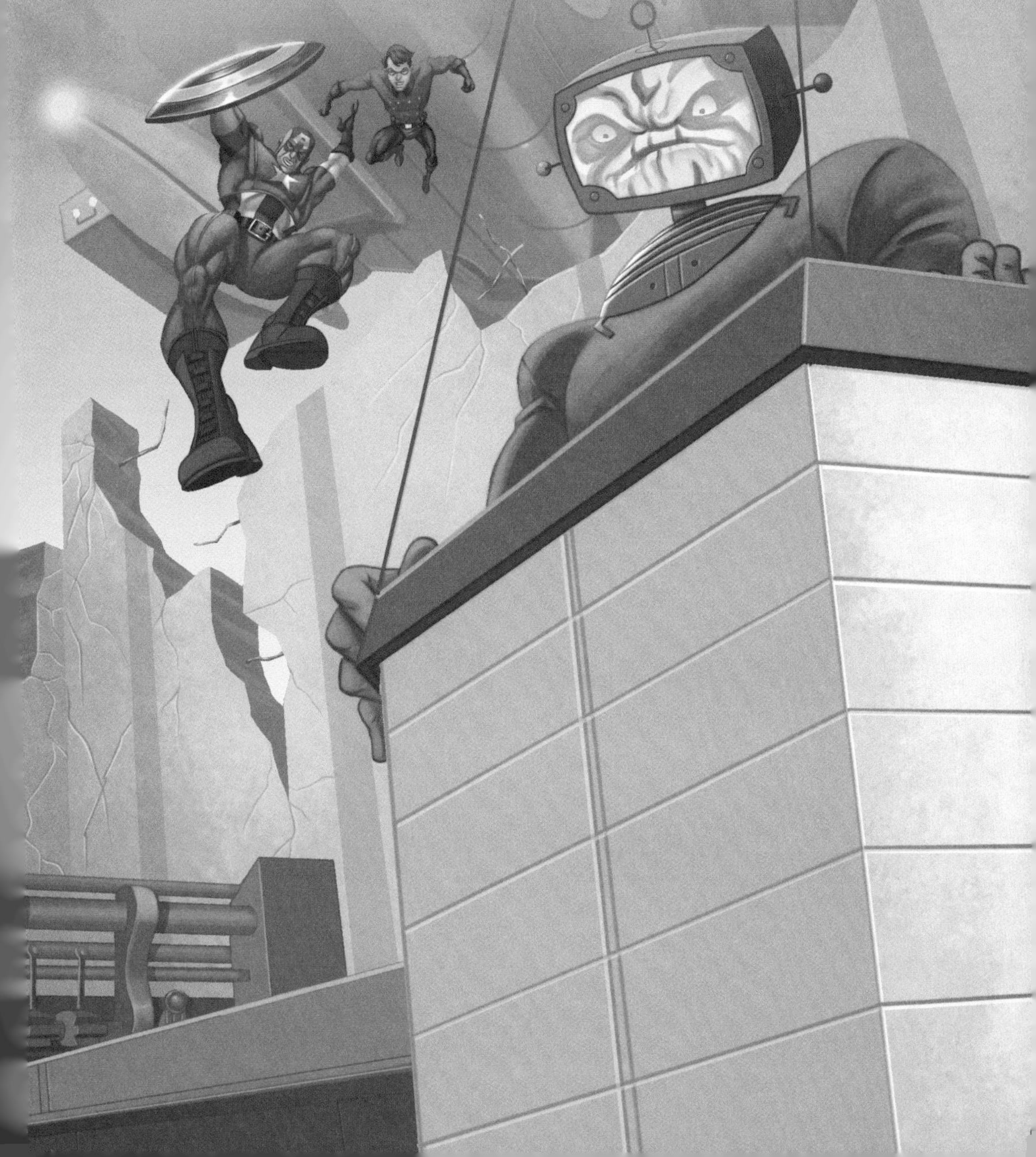

"You're a day late and a dollar short, Captain—my monster-men are more than a match for you," Arnim Zola replied. "Get them!"

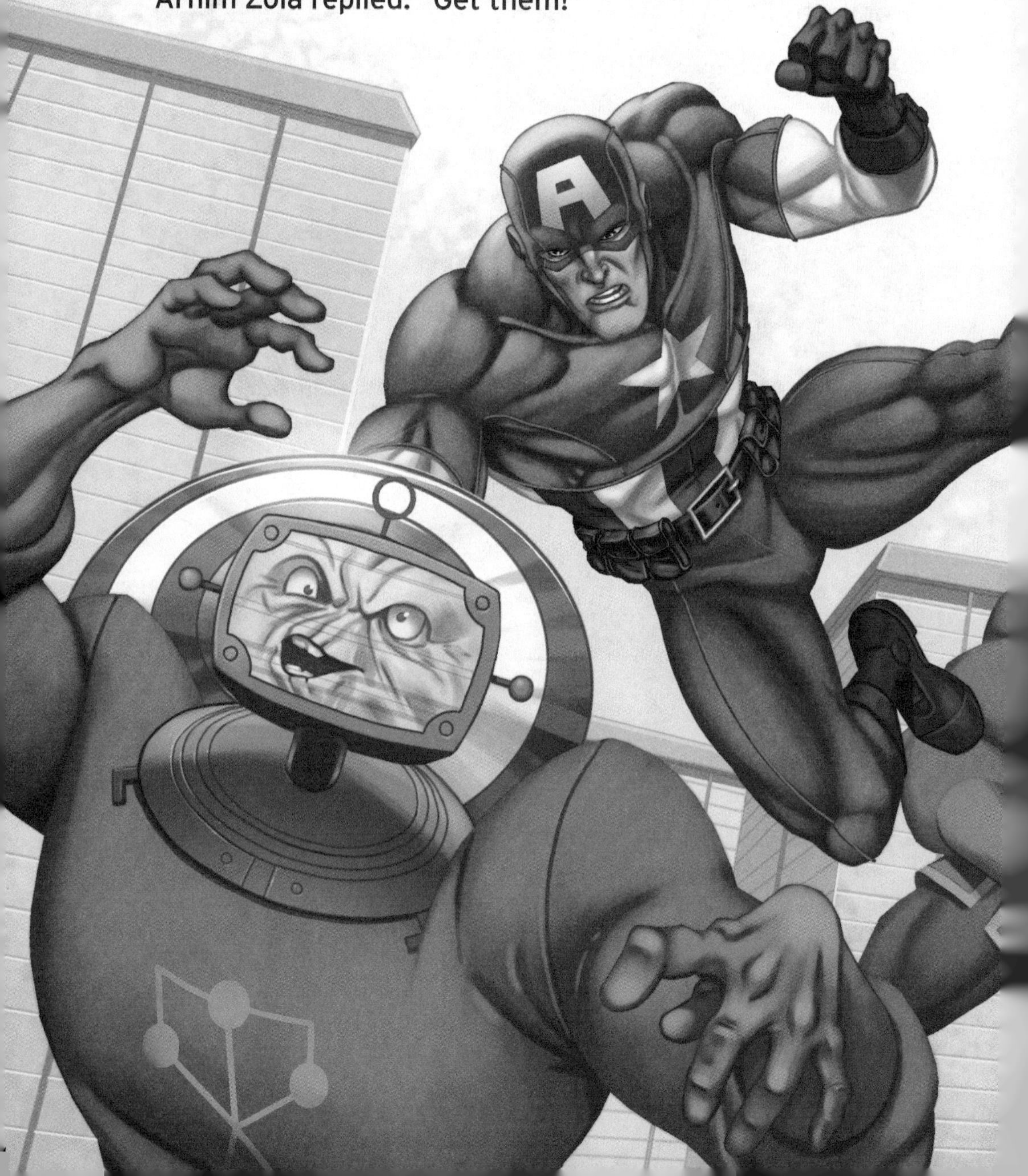

The monster-men lumbered forward.

"I hope this fight doesn't cost us an arm and a leg," Bucky joked.

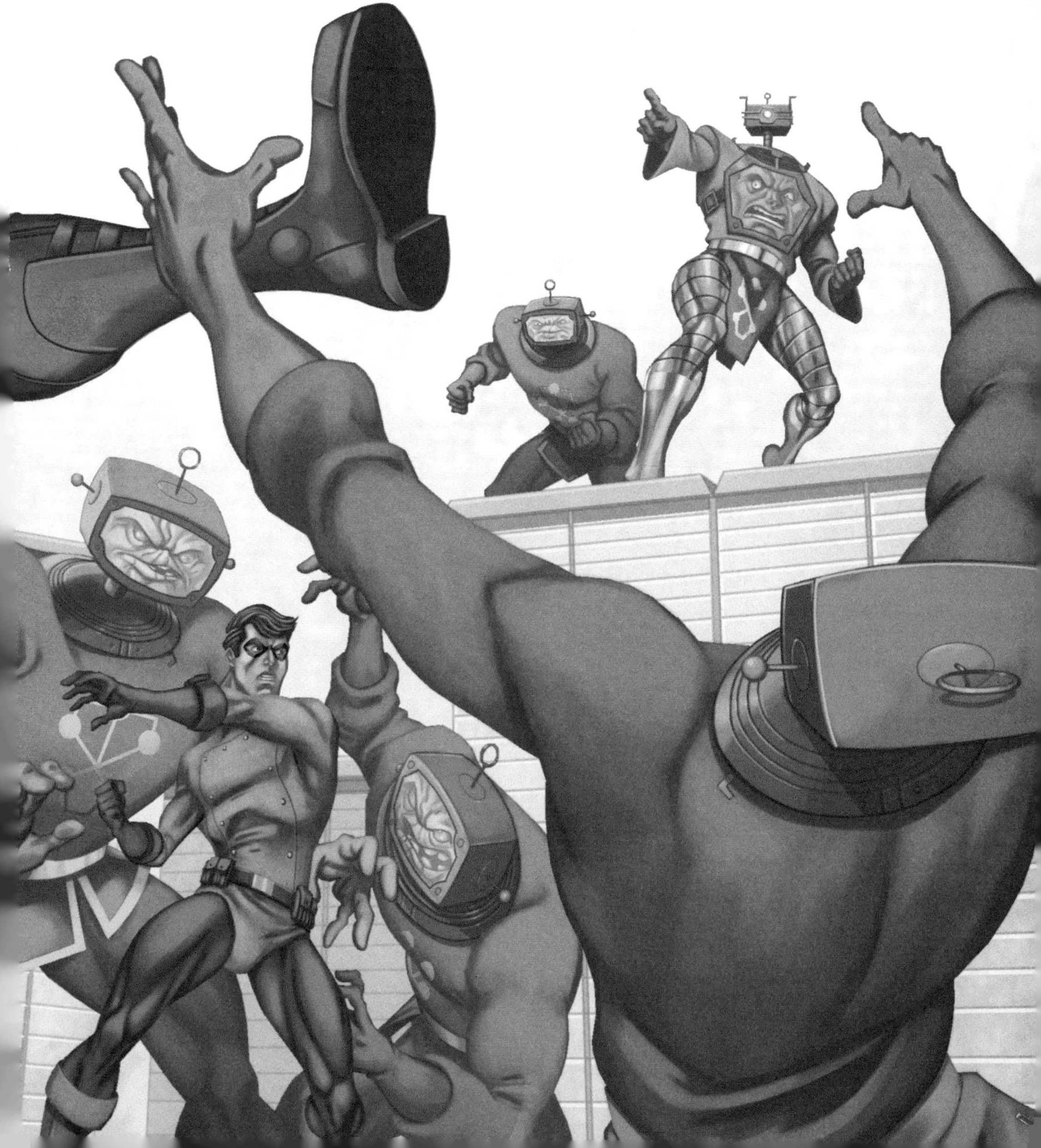

The monster-men were no match for Captain America and Bucky. Arnim Zola's creatures were strong, but the heroes were too fast and too skilled at fighting.

"Time to pay the piper, Zola!" Captain America said, stopping the last monster-man with his shield.

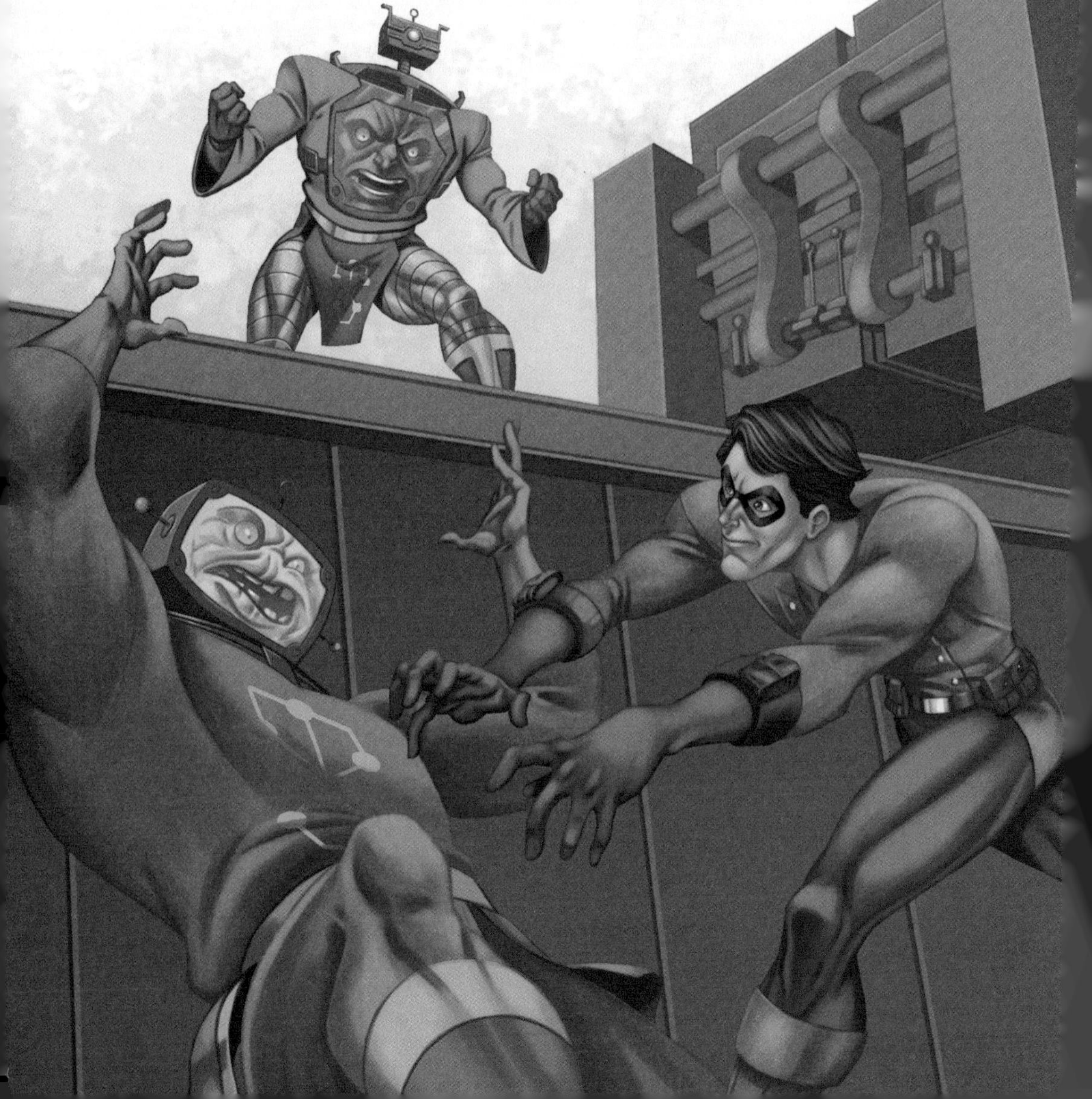

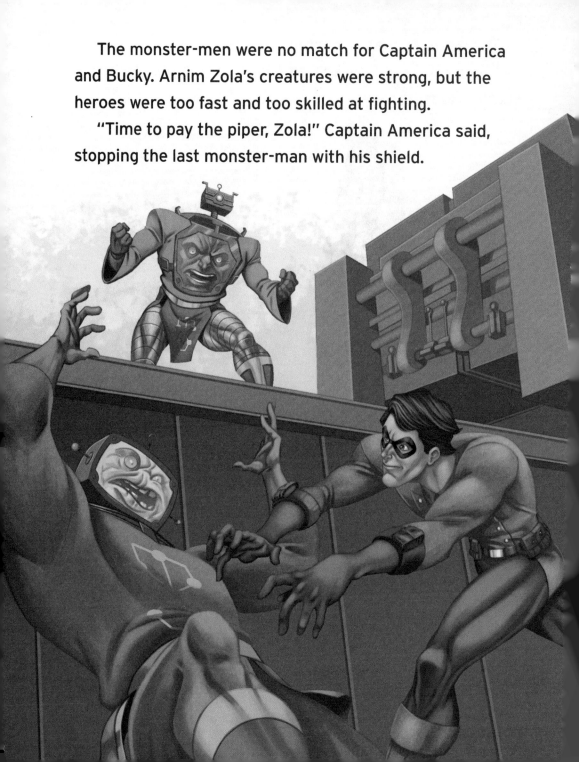

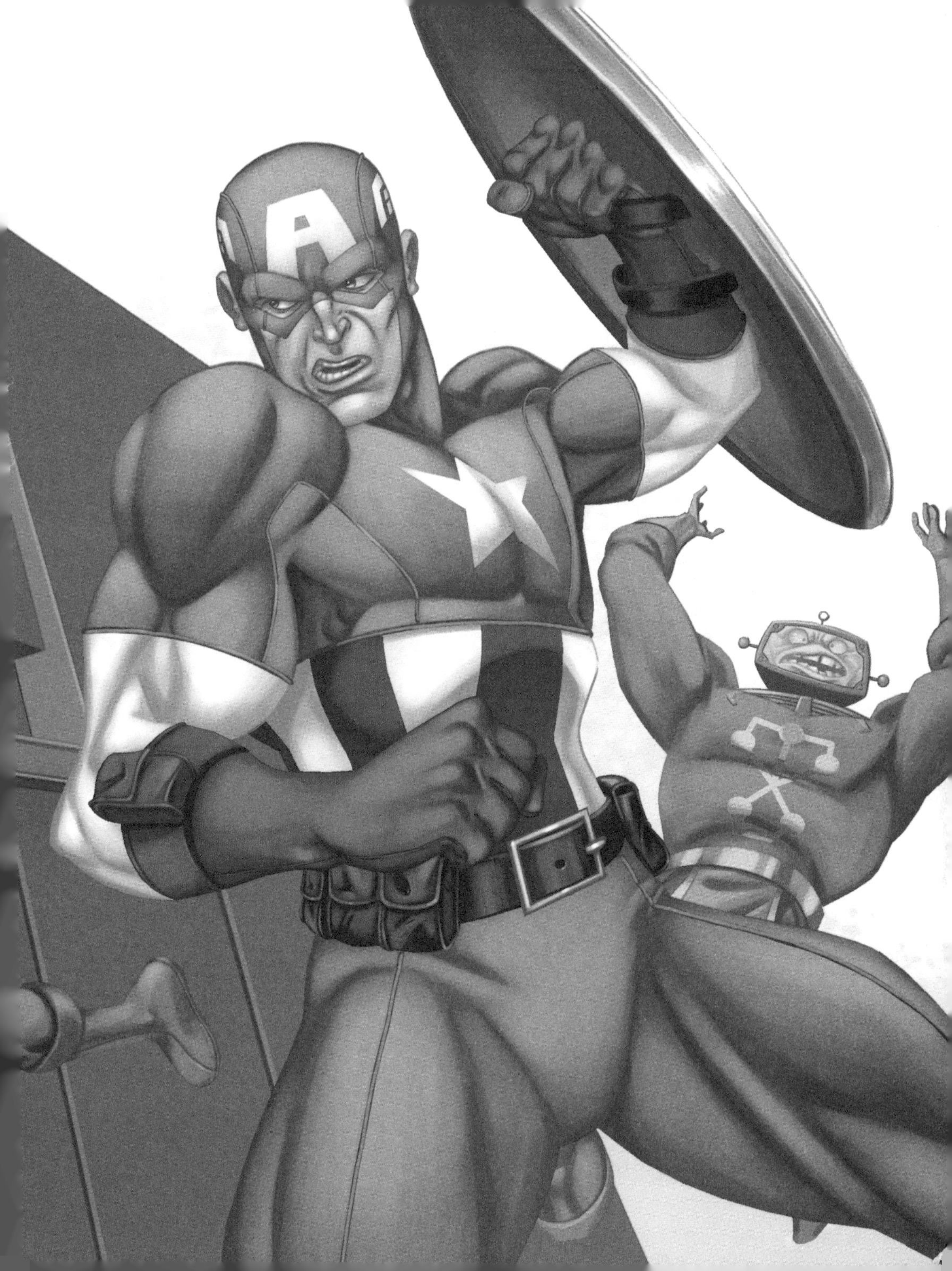

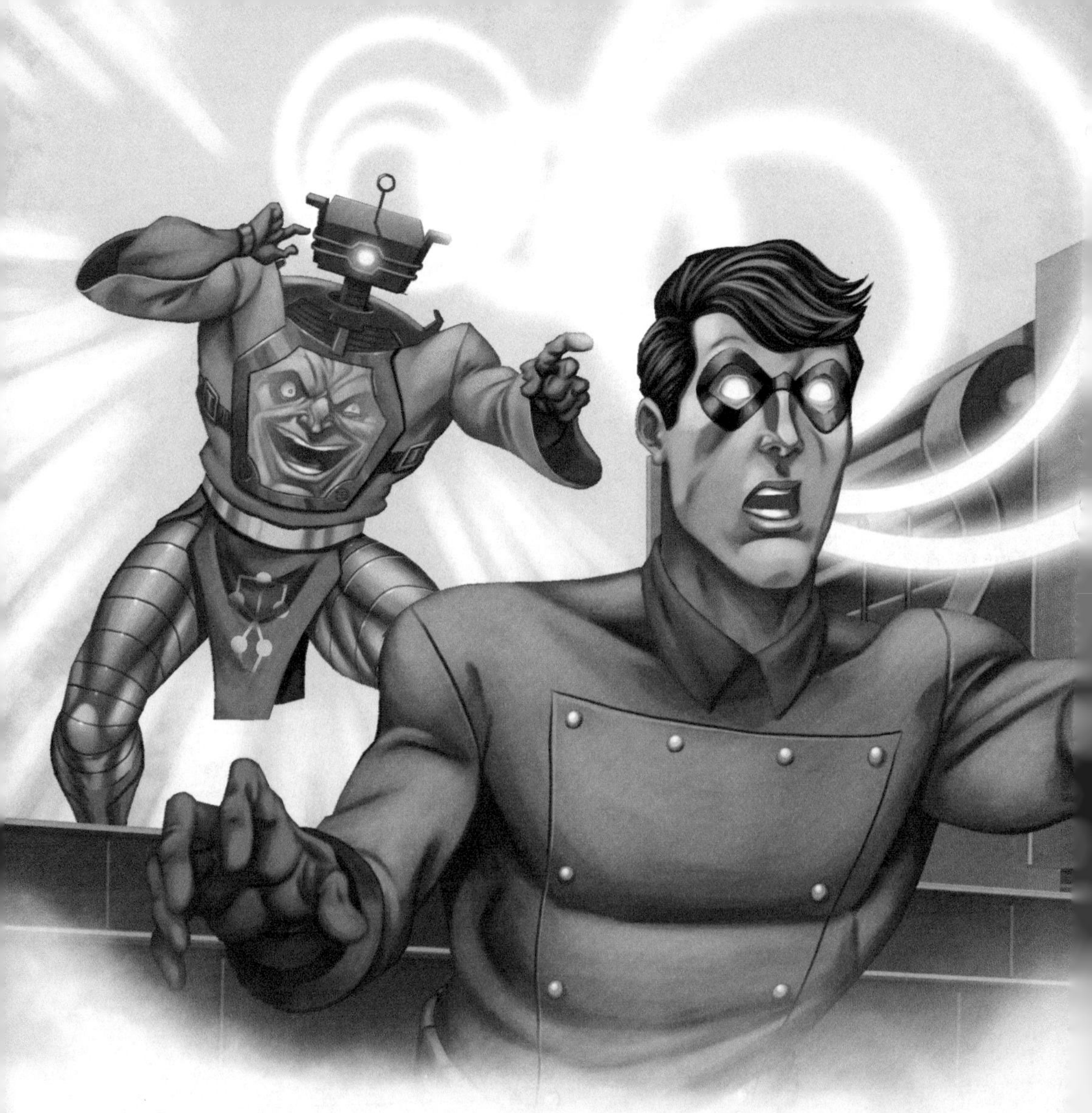

Without warning, Arnim Zola projected a powerful mind-control beam at Bucky. "There's one person you can't defeat," the villain said, laughing. "I will make your best friend your worst foe!"

The young hero's eyes turned white, and he began moving like a zombie toward Captain America!

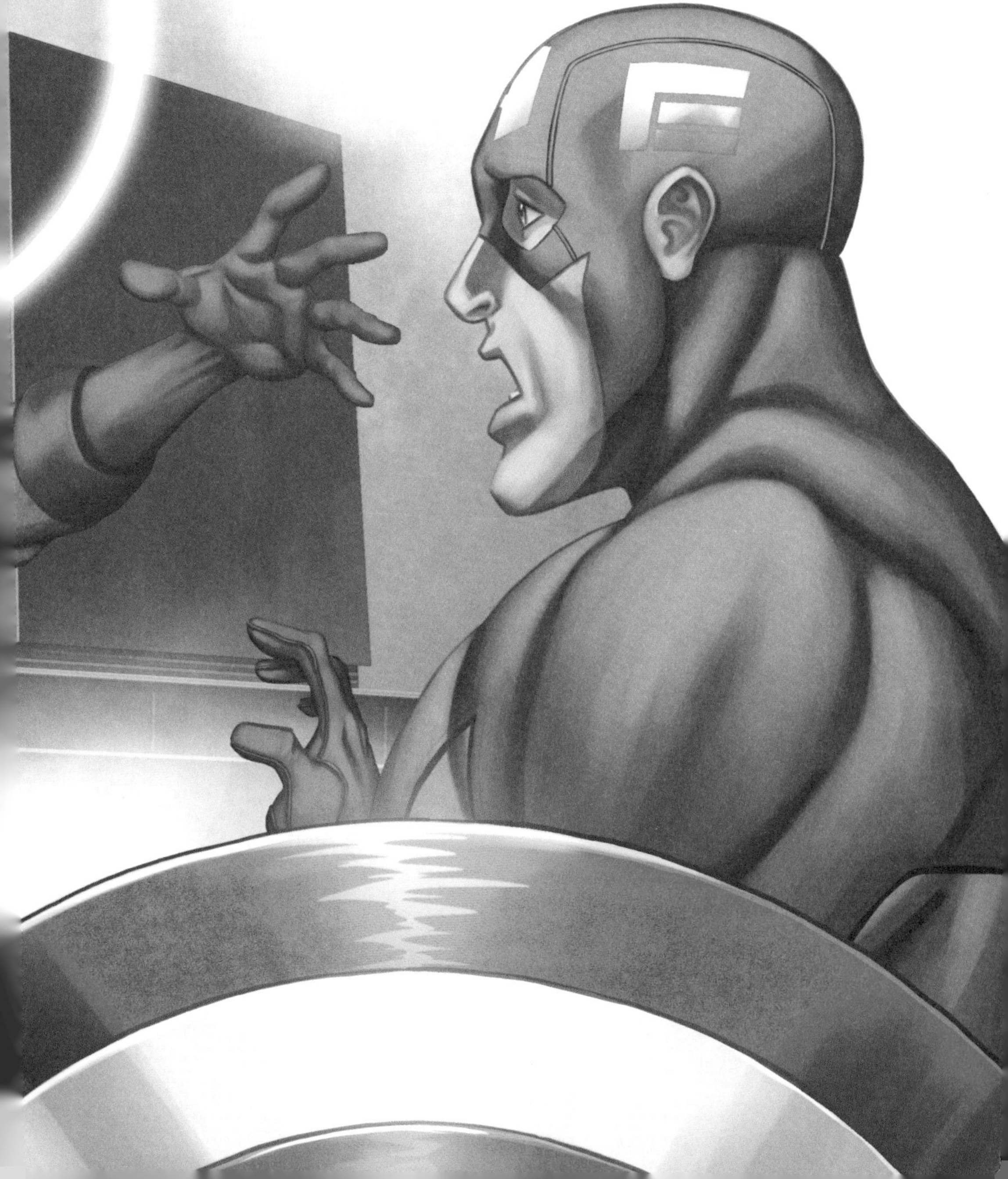

Bucky grabbed Captain America in a vise-like grip.

"Bucky, it's me, Cap!" the hero pleaded. He didn't want to hurt his friend. "We have to stop Zola!"

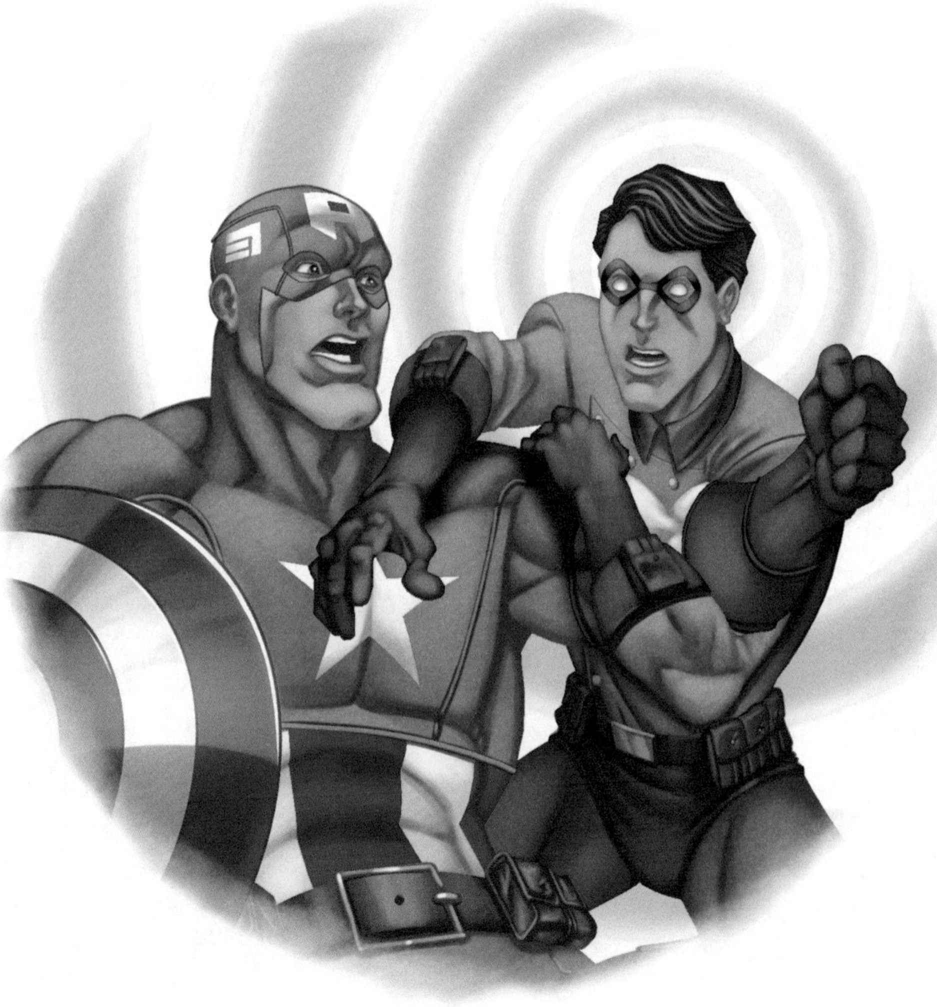

"With the mind-controlling powers of my ESP box," Zola bragged, "no one can stop me. Not even you, Captain America!"

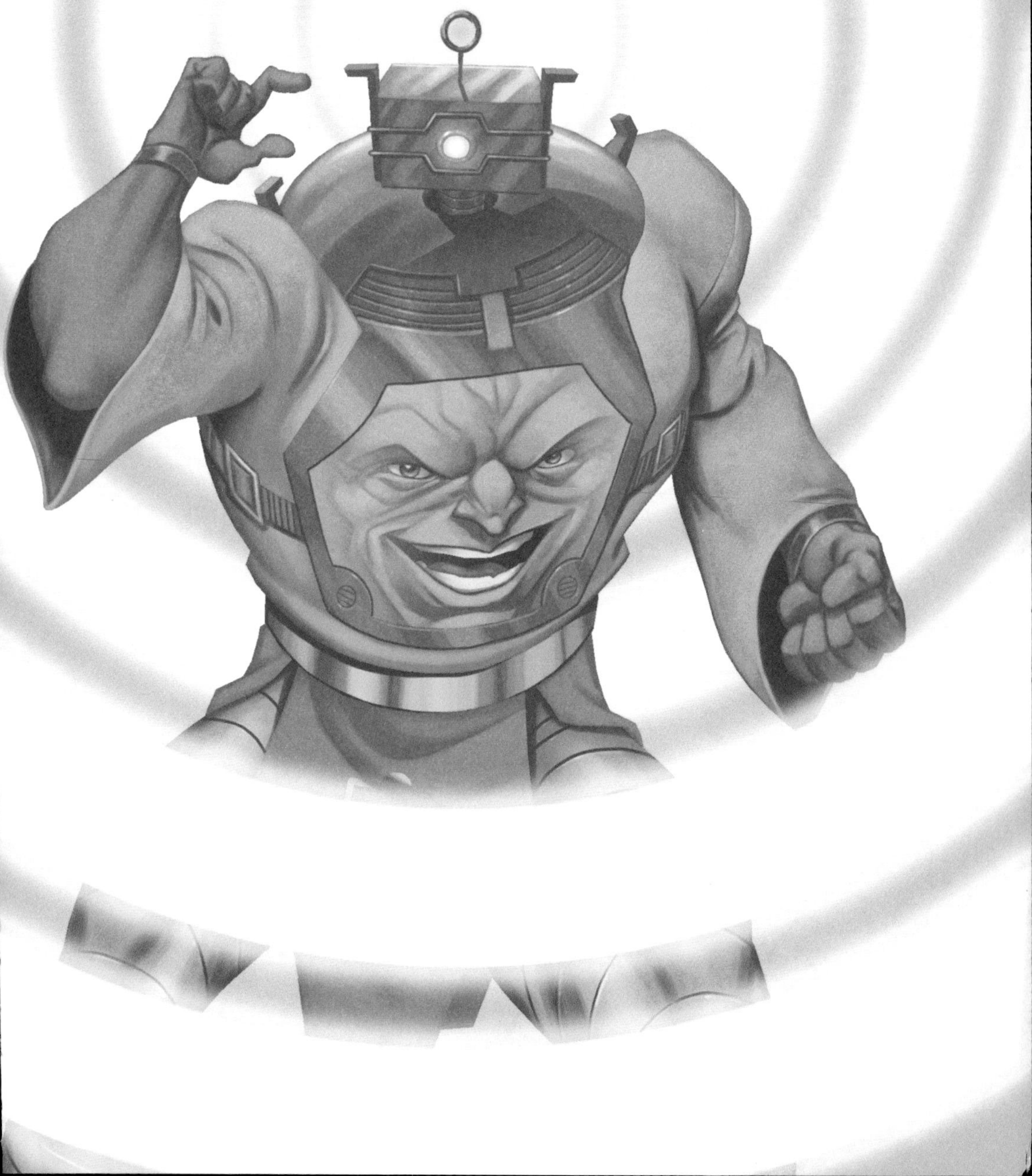

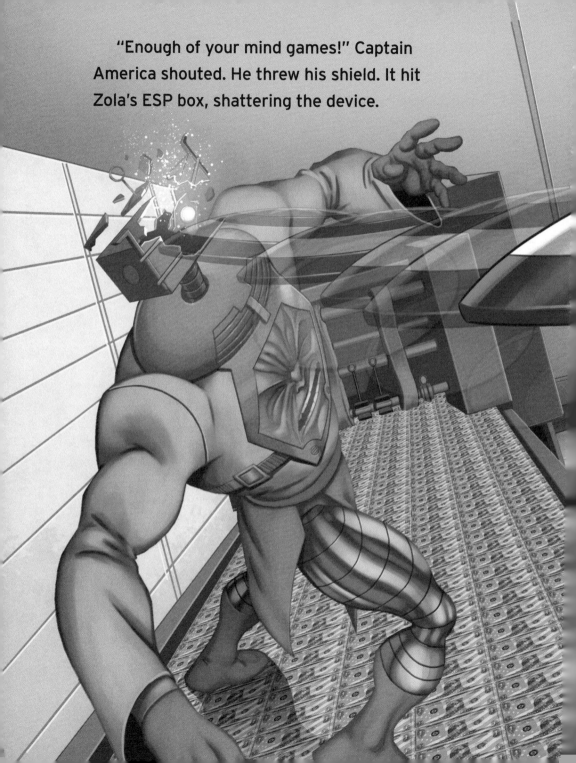

"Enough of your mind games!" Captain America shouted. He threw his shield. It hit Zola's ESP box, shattering the device.

Captain America's shield bounced off the villain and hit the printing press's controls. The machine roared to life!

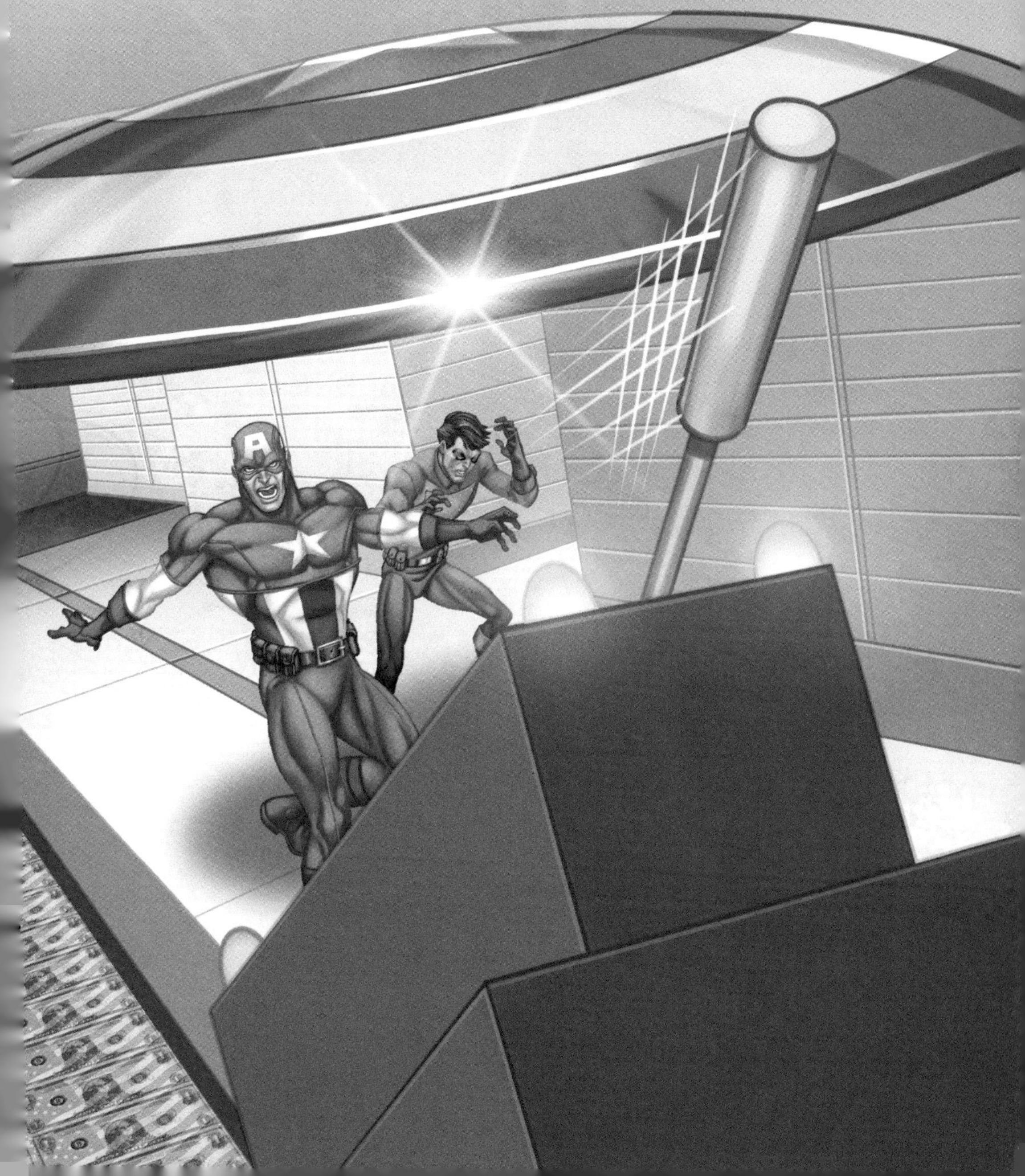

Arnim Zola's feet flew out from under him—

THUMP! —and he was sucked into the printing press!

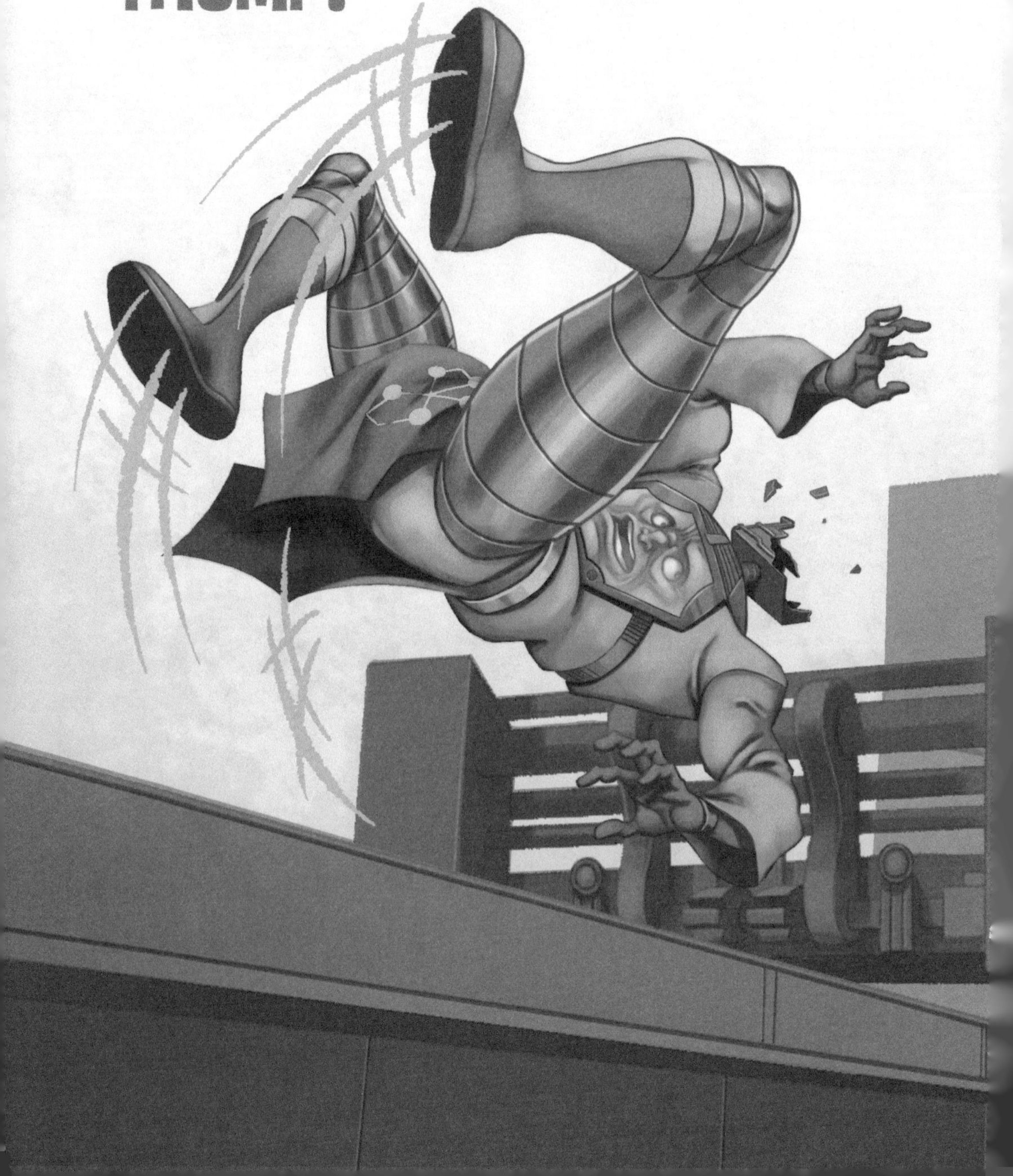

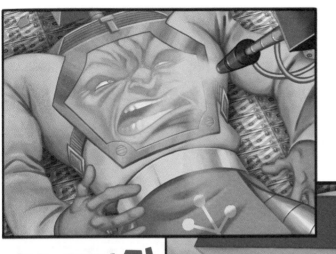

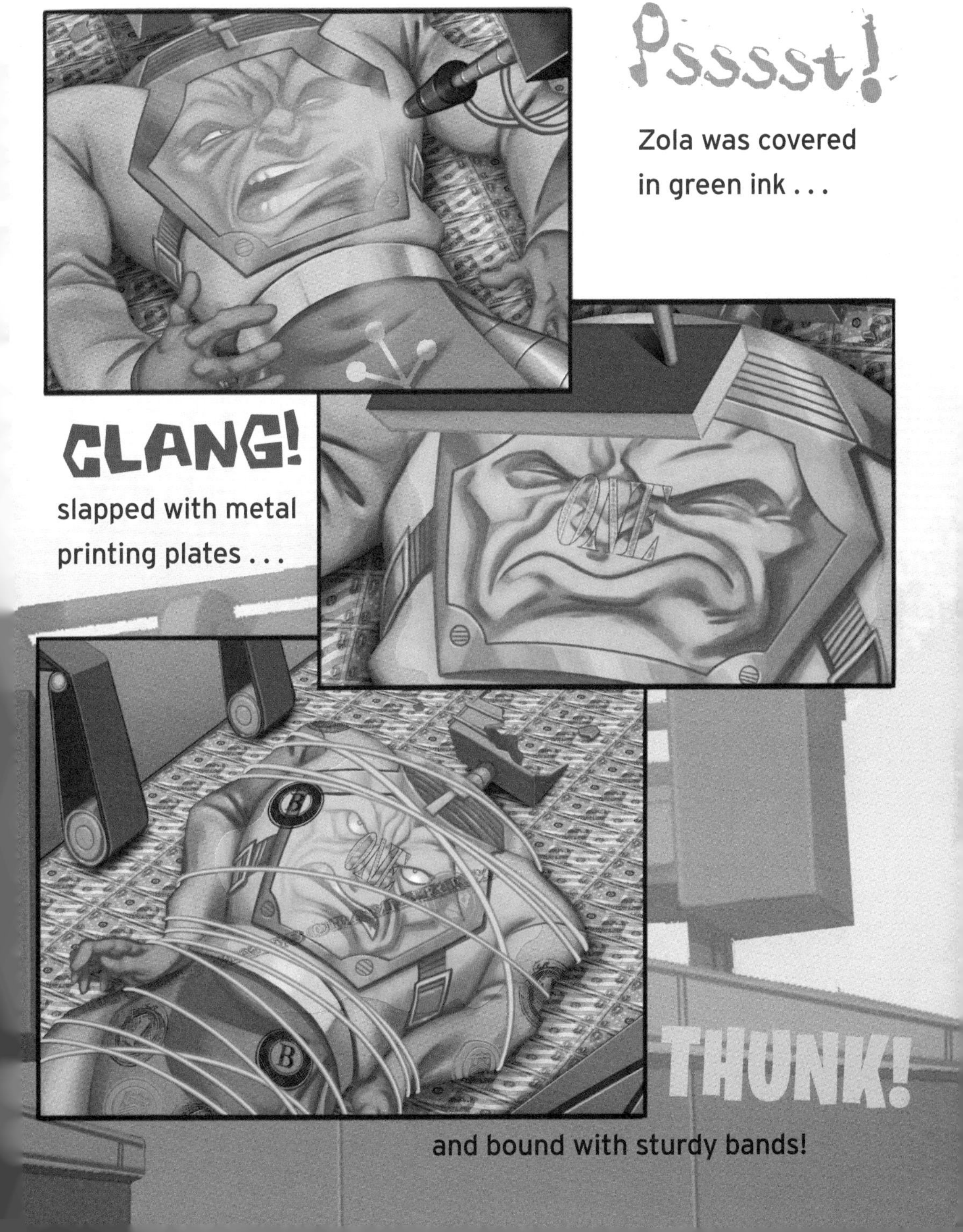

Psssst!

Zola was covered
in green ink . . .

CLANG!

slapped with metal
printing plates . . .

THUNK!

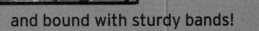

and bound with sturdy bands!

The printing press exploded! Colorful dollar bills rained down like confetti. Arnim Zola was defeated!

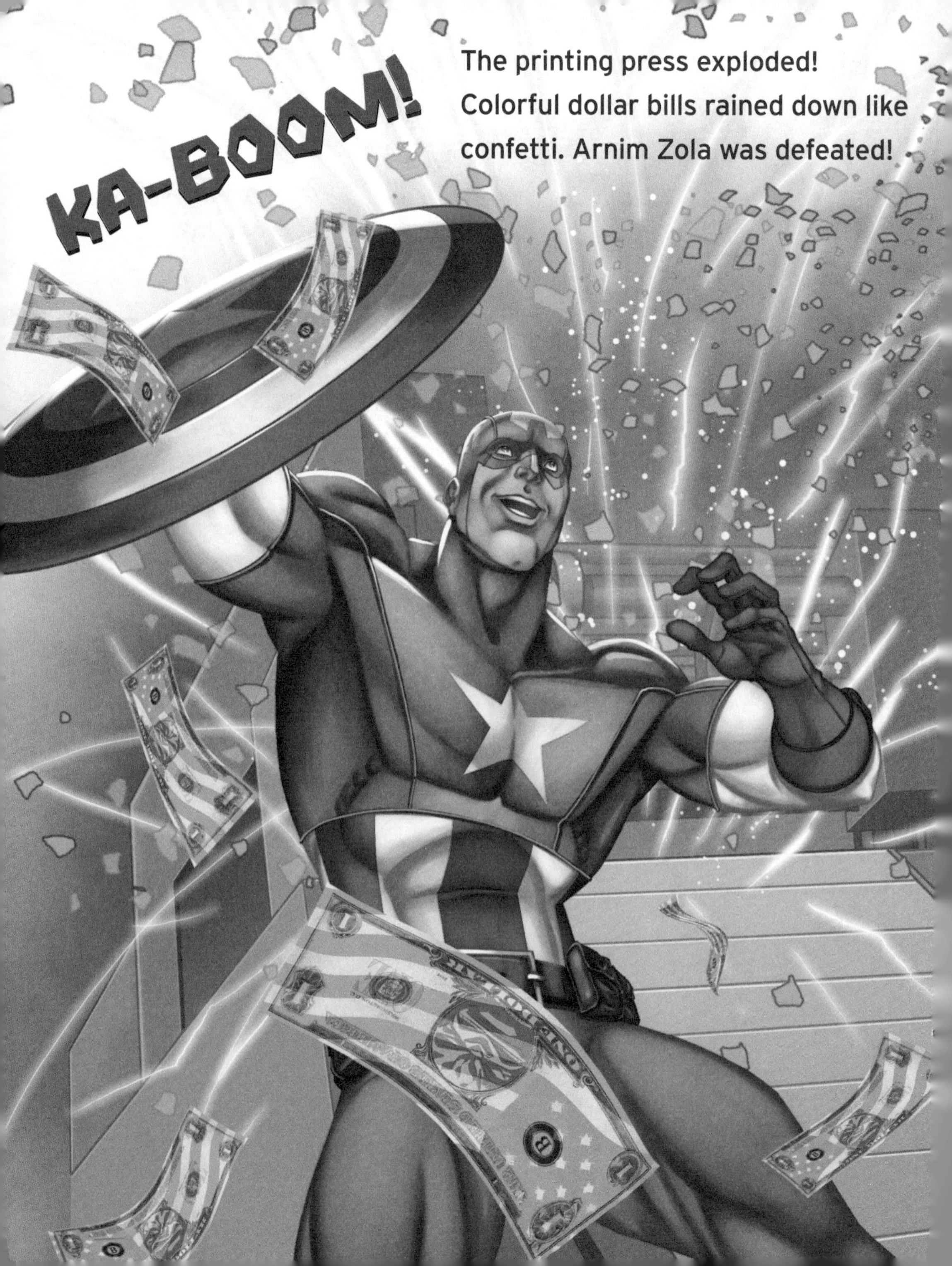
KA-BOOM!

Bucky unlocked the front door for the S.H.I.E.L.D. agents. Captain America handed the super villain over to them.

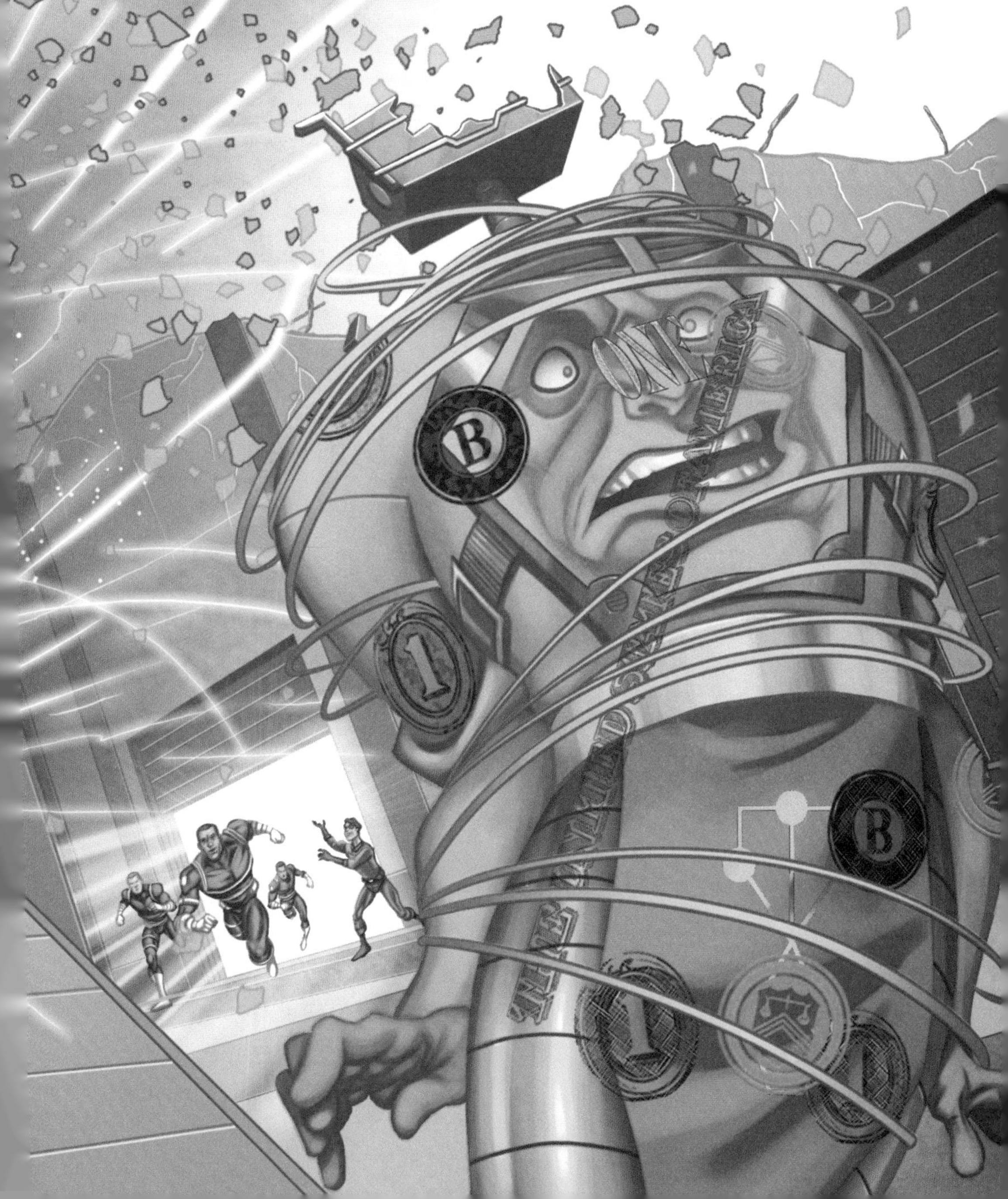

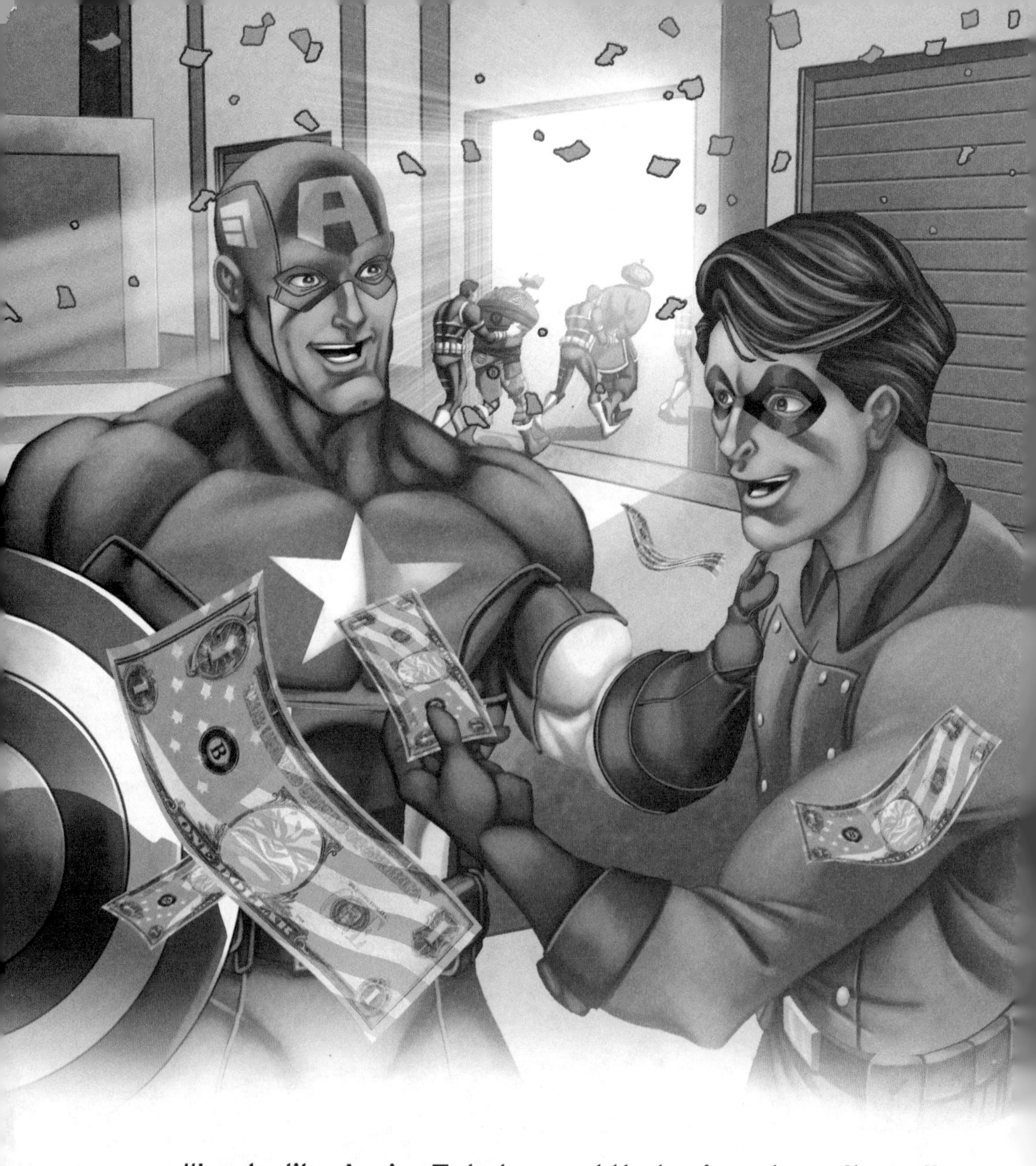

"Looks like Arnim Zola learned that crime doesn't pay," Captain America said as Bucky held up a dollar bill printed with Zola's face. "Now he's going to **spend** his time in jail."